THE REVENGE OF THE WHALE

AND OTHER STORIES

MARILYN SEWELL

FULLER PRESS
PORTLAND · OREGON

ANTHOLOGIES

Cries of the Spirit
Claiming the Spirit Within
Resurrecting Grace
Breaking Free: Women of Spirit at Midlife and Beyond

NONFICTION

Wanting Wholeness, Being Broken
Threatened with Resurrection
A Little Book on Forgiveness
A Little Book on Prayer
A Little Book of Reflections
Raw Faith: Following the Thread, a memoir

FICTION

In Time's Shadow: Stories About Impermanence

FILM

Marilyn is the subject of a documentary film, *Raw Faith*, directed by Peter Weidensmith. See the film at no charge at marilynsewell.com.

TABLE OF CONTENTS

PREFACE

I started writing in these short pieces quite by accident. Simply noticing and mentioning, that's all, and I kept discovering a culture increasingly shaky in terms of meaning and connection. I began to understand that we no longer have a cultural narrative in which we trust, or even one that makes much sense. Talking with a philosophy professor who is familiar with my work, I was surprised to learn that my little stories reflect the current reigning philosophy, postmodernism.

If you will allow me a quick and dirty definition: postmodernism posits that there is no objective reality—human understanding is a construct determined by social values, concepts, and language itself. Therefore, there is no truth. In fact, the word *post-truth* is now commonly used without a trace of irony.

It's not as though philosophers and other intellectuals sit around and make this stuff up—they are reflecting what they see when they note the assumptions about meaning indicated by the thinking and behavior of people in a given culture. In other words, postmodernism is the water we swim in, not something we choose or do not choose. It's what has come to be, what *is*.

Metanarratives which give structure and meaning to our lives are now considered passe, and those who believe in them, naïve. God flew the coop long ago, and so have science, technology, and obviously, government. Reason and logic are simply tools of the ruling class. Your story is simply your story, and not to be generalized upon, and mine is mine. Ergo, my truth is as good as yours, for there is no measure, no authority. There is no common humanity, no *us*.

People who've never read a word about postmodernism are now living it. So, I have discovered, are my fictional characters. They are lost, they are lonely, they search for love and meaning and generally come up short.

Why was I drawn to writing about these people? They are, after all, thoroughly ordinary people. Like myself. Looking for God (or a god) in all the wrong places. Wondering if they'll stumble across the meaning of their life before they die. No heroics here. I'm writing about them because each one echoes a part of me—that which yearns, that which is unfinished, that which despairs of finding answers, direction.

A cursory look at my stories showed me how thoroughly immersed I am in this culture of disconnect, how closely I identify with these people who wander off-balance in an increasingly hostile, confusing world. My characters:

—judge others as being wrong or unworthy.

—long for connection, but miss one another in passing.

—see logic as an encumbrance.

—fear death, but several choose suicide, in one form or another.

—perceive rules and regulations as being arbitrary.

—buy stuff and more stuff and feel burdened by it, but can't stop.

—cling to behavior that has not delivered joy or peace of mind.

—trust in alternative sources of knowing.

—have expectations that are always being turned upside down.

How can I not love these people? I'm like Holden Caulfield, the unreliable narrator in *The Catcher in the Rye*, who says, "I'm standing on the edge of some crazy cliff. What I have to do, I have to catch everybody if they start to go over the cliff—I mean if they're running and they don't look where they're going I have to come out from somewhere and catch them. That's all I'd do all day. I'd just be the catcher in the rye and all."

So here they are, running and running and not looking where they're going. They really are doing the best they can. *Aren't we?*

I. LOVE

Ah, it is the animating force of the universe! It appears in many forms, often in disguise. It is the source of our greatest joy and one of the most common forms of our undoing.

TREE OF LIFE

She's coming in today/ I feel a hard-on coming already/ oh, shit, I hate myself for this/ my dick has a mind of its own/ mind-less,really/ should have been honest the first session:/ can't do this, I have the hots for you, Darlin'/ or something more professional/ like Thanks for considering me as your therapist/ but I don't think we are a good match/ yeah, that's it, something cool not cruel/ can't blame her, in any case/ not her fault my hands got sweaty/ the first thirty seconds after she stepped into my office/ hazel eyes cast down/ ass fighting her jeans/ breasts pulling against the buttons on her white cotton shirt/ candy lips.

Oh, how I wanted her that first day/ three months later, it's worse/ she's invading my prayers, my dreams/ I wake up in a sweat/ night taking me into her arms, her body/ uncanny the hold/ not like I want to screw every pretty woman I see, no/ Caroline, that's her name/ her Southern accent, oh/ my growing-up days in Georgia/ forever gone/ she's the apple in my garden.

This wild itch/ this glittering lust/ at my age/ who would have thought it/ married to Mary/ happy the way good marriages are happy/ held by history, contained by kin/ it's not that I want an affair/ ruining all I have built/ all I am/ I'll tell her today/ make up some paltry excuse/ bow out, let her go/ yeah, back to breakfast cereal/ negotiating traffic in my Prius/ email, my emotional hit for the day/ goddamn television at night, oh yeah.

Hi, Caroline! Come on in/ What's going on with you today/ I see/ of course, I'll be there for you/ why would you doubt that/ I'm not going anywhere/ you're my reason for being/ I mean, for being here in the office each day/ you and my other clients/ now, tell me more.

WHAT HOLDS ME

I wake each morning full of the fragments of dreams,
Lost and alone.
I make coffee,
Pour the whole-grain cereal and the low-fat milk.
I eat and drink,
Thinking that I will come alive
If I do those things living people do.
I read the paper:
—a young soldier has died from a roadside bomb, his fiancée mourns
—a bride in India has been set ablaze, her dowry insufficient
—a father's car has slid on ice, his seven-year-old son is dead in freezing water
What holds me here,
On this fragile, disappointing earth?
The space they left:
The figure, the pattern, breath of all that has gone,
What has been, remains for me.

MANSPLAINING

I said to him, "Let's have lunch by the lake."
He said, "It's not a lake, it's a river."
I said, "Our picnic will not know the difference."

CALI

based on a letter in the *Oregonian*

Cali (short for Mexicali Rose), a miniature horse, is the service animal for Mona Ramouni, who has been blind since shortly after birth. Ramouni's parents, devout Muslims, refused her a dog, because they consider dogs unclean. "I would not trade her for 10 dogs," says Ramouni. She reports that Cali likes to watch TV, eat pizza, and roll around in mud. Cali is a real people magnet, says Ramouni.

Thanks to a letter-writing campaign to the Department of Justice, mounted by Ramouni and others, miniature horses have received ADA approval as service animals. These horses are very smart and can be house trained. They live 2 or 3 times as long as a dog.

One drawback: they need quite a large room to gallop in.

THE DANCER

Once upon a time there was a girl who danced. She had long slender arms and hands that moved like water, legs that were strong and lean and held her body well: she seemed to be part of the earth, yet somehow floating above it.

Father gone, her mother said, Go, child, if you can, and make something of yourself. So the girl left home at 13, her formal education complete, and joined a dance troupe.

She danced before admiring throngs in cities all over the country. Although she was one among many beautiful women, she had the darkest hair and the brightest eyes of all. She kept company with many a handsome fellow, but was never tempted to give her heart away, for she felt sure that the one she was meant to marry would appear one day. Faithful to that dream, she was content to wait, filled with the love of every good thing that life could give, whether it was a winsome song or the spring rain.

As the years passed, she grew only more beautiful and more adept at her art. She became the featured dancer of her company, and her name appeared on marquees outside theatres, her picture in advertisements and newspaper reviews. She loved the city lights and all the pleasures afforded her.

Then a long hardship fell upon the land, and there was little work to be found. Many who had been prosperous became poor, some became desperate to feed their families. People could no longer pay to see dancers, for that seemed frivolous in such a time. The music stopped, the dancing stopped, and the woman who danced knew that her life would be changing.

Though the times were perilous, women still wished to be thought attractive, so the dancer who no longer danced found a job selling hair curlers in the nation's capital, a busy crowded city full of other job-seekers like herself. She missed her friends in the dance troupe. She missed the bright lights. Most of all, she missed the dancing. She did well selling, because she liked people, and she liked to laugh—of course her lovely dark hair was the best advertisement of all. Customers joked and talked with her and before they knew it, they were buying hair curlers, thinking to have hair like this seller of curlers.

The dancer who no longer danced was still young, still beautiful. She carried herself like a queen—a strange queen, perhaps, selling hair curlers, but even bankers were selling peanuts on the street. She did what she had to do, sending money when she could back home to her mother and two younger sisters.

She took what simple joys her life would allow—she went to the cinema now and then and went for a soda with her workmates. But she was lonely. She missed her sisters, who lived in a faraway city, and she continued to miss the friends she had toured with, who by that time had scattered across the country. She missed the stage, where she had been able to give her gifts so freely. Sometimes at night she put on her ballet slippers and danced in front of her mirror, feeling the old passions rise within. But a gift not given begins to turn back on itself, so after a while, she stopped this practice, put the shoes away.

Being of German descent, this woman went each day at noon to a German restaurant, the Old Heidelburg, where she could get a substantial plate of food for a reasonable price, and where the sounds and smells reminded her of the home she had left so long ago. She always sat alone, reading or thinking. Months passed, winter fell upon the land, the city turned white with snow. Shivering in her cloth coat, she felt lost and alone.

A few days before Christmas, a man appeared, a waiter. Handsome and gentle in manner, he was from a town far south. He, too, had come to the city for the opportunity to work. He waited on her that day, and thereafter every time she appeared. With an easy smile, he sometimes brought her streusel or hot apple cider to fend off the cold. So in the midst of the coldest part of the year, she began to find warmth and pleasure.

She found herself drawn to this man as she had never been drawn to any other. Was this the one she had been waiting for? Strange, to find him in a restaurant— and stranger still to find a man from the South, who spoke with such a strange accent. Still, his words were soft and pleasing to her ear. He was a man of the land, who all his life had worked with his hands. He had a strong body made just the way a man's body should be made. He teased her and made her laugh. She realized that she had not laughed so much for a long while.

These two young people had little money. They ate at the Old Heidelburg, went for long walks in the wintry city, once in a while attended a matinee. They went swimming in the heated city pool, her dark hair tucked under a cap, her body at one with the water. The first time she saw him dive off the high board, she knew she loved him. He sprang up and out and then down, in a perfect swan dive, cutting through the water with scarcely a splash. With his arms spread wide, embracing the air as they did, he reminded her of a magnificent bird.

Everything seemed filled with light when they were together. No matter that they had so little in the way of material things. He thought she was gorgeous, no matter what she put on—she walked as though she owned the world. He was always there for her, always smiling when he approached, letting her know by his mien that he couldn't imagine being without her. When he touched her, her breathing slowed, her fear left, she felt that something partial had been made whole.

One fine day they were in the park—spring had found its way once again to the earth, and the cherry blossoms were dancing upon the trees. A couple came by with a baby in a carriage, and soon a conversation ensued. Eventually the dancer and her Southern man were allowed to hold the child, who cooed and gurgled as happy babies do. The infant seemed comfortable and satisfied, being passed around to strangers this way. She and her man were smitten. That very evening they decided to marry and have babies of their own. Which, before too long, they did.

Regretfully, I cannot end my tale here. I would like to tell you that the story ends happily ever after, as we are all hoping. But that would not be the truth. You see, these two were as star-crossed as lovers could ever be.

She was a city girl, born and bred, and he was a Louisiana boy who could not live apart from the land. They moved first to the northern city of her youth. Finding work only in a candy factory, he began to die a slow death there on the factory floor, so took to drink to assuage his pain. He entreated his love to move to the small town where he grew up, where he could be close to the earth and his people, and she finally agreed. But there she found only isolation and boredom. She felt her difference, felt her spirit grow faint.

I will spare you the details: they include unfaithfulness, mental illness, alcoholism, and divorce. Though the man was to marry four more times before his death, his eyes always filled with tears when he spoke of her. As for her, she could never look at another man. She died first, in the city in which she was born, over a period of years, of cancer. He died ten years later, in a state mental hospital in Louisiana, of alcohol dementia. For the previous three years, he was unable to recognize his own three children. His children, and hers.

Still, neither time nor distance nor suffering could make them forget. Though apart for the final thirty years of their lives, each always fell into sorrow at the mention of the other. As she neared death, she spoke his name. After his death, his social worker sent his personal effects to his children. I am the eldest. I found among his paltry belongings a carefully kept photo, still in the studio folder. It was the dancer, in a tutu, balanced on one toe, her other leg reaching to the sky, her arms spread as if to contain all the joy in the world.

   —In memory of my parents, Marion and James

THINGS MY HUSBAND DOES THAT IRRITATE ME

—snores and accuses me of same, which I am sure is not true
—slurps his coffee, though not loudly
—reads news stories aloud to me at breakfast, when I am trying to read my own stories
—never says "I'm sorry," like when he knocks over a glass of red wine, says "Whoops" instead
—never says "Oh, my God, I could have hit him!" when he comes close to hitting a cyclist, says "Whoops" instead
—when I say I don't understand, repeats, only louder
—wanders around as if in a daze, says "Hmmmm, that's interesting" when he misplaces his keys or his cell phone, meaning, How could this item disappear into another space-time continuum?
—accelerates when approaching a red light, presumably optimistic that the light will turn green
—parks the car, locks it, leaves, walks back several blocks to check if it's locked

—punches the elevator button multiple times, to be sure it hears him

—explains things in which I have no interest, like how machines work or how concrete is properly poured

—consults his cell phone for directions, though he knows the route, while I wait, trapped in my seat belt

—gets only $20 each time he visits the ATM, later asks me if I have cash

— wants some of the same late-night snack I fix for myself

—imitates mating sounds of birds when we are in a park or wilderness area, sometimes they answer

—insists on being cheerful, even when the weather is gloomy, and I am depressed

—tells me I am not overweight, which I know I am, thus making me doubt his judgment

—treats boring people as if they were interesting, thus encouraging more of their unfortunate self-expression

— is charming and attentive to people I don't like

— has ingratiated himself with my friends, who now like him better than me

DADDY'S GIRL

Martha didn't want to go home. She knew before she walked through the front door what she would find—her father would be drunk. *Same old story since Mom died.* She decided to take the chance that things might be different this time. They weren't.

Her dad was watching a football game, and yes, drunk. Room littered with newspapers, discarded clothing, beer bottles. Stale smoke of cigarettes wafting through the air.

Martha said, "Daddy, turn off the TV." He did; something was up. She and her young man stood side by side. Martha spoke in a clipped voice. "Daddy, this is John." She hesitated. "We're going to be married."

Her father looked up through blurry blue eyes, lost for long seconds. Tears slowly gathered, he began to cry uncontrollably, face in his hands. "John, John, my baby girl! Be good to her. Be good to my baby."

GRACE L. KENNY

(1923-2014)
a found poem[*]

Grace always read the obituaries.
She cut out those
of the people she knew
and saved them.
Now she has one of her own.
Grace grew up on small farms,
at one time living in a one-room shack.
This upbringing
taught her to be frugal with her lifestyle,
but very generous with her family.
She lived in town with relatives
while attending high school
and after a very short career with Southwest Bell,
met and married Fred Rau in 1944.
Their son, Fred, was born in December 1944,
and Grace's husband died
in the Battle of the Bulge in January 1945.
On a trip to Oregon to visit her late husband's family,
Grace met Jack Krafsic,

---

[*] These words were taken unchanged, from an obituary column
in the *Oregonian*.

who incidentally was an acquaintance of her first husband.
Grace put in her years as a first-class mom and housewife
        until 1961
when Jack passed away.
Undaunted by the loss of two husbands,
Grace married Lawrence Kenney,
incidentally an acquaintance of her second husband, Jack,
and began her life on a Sherman County wheat and
        cattle ranch.
Grace loved her children, grandchildren, great-
        grandchildren, dogs,
baking, gardening, the beach, the Seattle Mariners, the
        limited amount
of travel she was able to do, and in later years, the
        occasional martini.
She was Swedish, and despite that,
had a good sense of humor.
She passed away February 18, 2014,
two days after her 91st birthday.
Grace had a good life
and gave a good life to her husbands and family.
Her philosophy of life could be expressed as
she accepted the few bad times with the many good times
with a quote by one of her favorite newsmen,
        Walter Cronkite,
"And that's the way it is."

BECOMING A BODHISATTVA

I've been reading some Buddhist books, and so instead of making so many New Year resolutions, I decided to make one big one, a Buddhist vow called the Bodhisattva Vow—a commitment to keep my heart open and to show compassion to all sentient beings. Sentient would include Ray, the boyfriend who dumped me six months ago, that I hate and can't forget. And my next-door neighbor who parks his truck in front of my house and who chains his dog to a post. And the minister at my church who has a bad haircut and whose sermons are deadly boring. And whoever it was who broke into my house and left muddy tracks on my blue carpet and stole my camera and the pearl necklace my grandmother gave me. All of these I have to love, and more. Can't even stop with humans. Have to stop eating veal, eat only free-range chickens not harmed before they are killed.

Probably can't keep this Bodhisattva vow, but the book said nobody keeps it perfectly, you just have to have the intention. You're supposed to start with giving love and compassion to yourself. I can't do that, so I'm going to start with the chickens, next my neighbor, then the minister, then the thief. And last to Ray. Maybe then I can love myself. And forgive myself for being so unlovable.

KENNETH AND HELEN[*]

Kenneth and Helen eloped on February 20, 1944,
and were never apart
in their 70 years of marriage.
They even held hands while eating breakfast.
Helen died at 92, on April 12, 2014.
Daughter Cody reported
that after Helen died,
Kenneth, age 91, looked at his children,
said, "Mom's dead,"
and quickly began to decline.
He died the next morning.
In their obituary,
Kenneth and Helen appear in a 1941 photo,
a remarkably handsome couple
sitting on the front bumper of an ancient car,
holding hands,
smiling broadly enough
to light up the world.

———————————

* story taken from an obituary

THE MOST HATED HOLIDAY

I read an article today that said Valentine's Day is the most hated holiday. I understand that. My bad feelings about Valentine's started in the first grade, in Miss Cady's class, when we all made valentines and passed them out to our classmates. Some people got 20, others got 12 or 14, I got 6, and one of those was from Miss Cady.

If you are alone on Valentine's Day, which I usually am, you feel like you're missing out, like everyone in the world except you has a sweetheart, the sweetheart is taking them out for dinner, with champagne, probably giving them a gift, too, maybe a single red rose in a long white box or a special piece of jewelry. You go to the mailbox that day, you hope someone has sent you a valentine, that happens, but it's from your sister, which is okay, but you've never been all that fond of your sister. Or it could be from a man, a friend of yours who wants to be more than a friend, but unfortunately has lips you would not kiss, under any circumstances.

Maybe when February 14 rolls around you're in a

relationship you don't want to be in, you are just waiting for the right time to break it off, a holiday is not a good time. You're uncomfortable, soon you'll be telling him you never want to see him again, really puts a damper on a romantic evening. He may even give you a gift, you will not want it, as it came from him, not from somebody you could be in love with. You like to think of yourself as kind, so you don't want to hurt him by rejecting his gift, you're already anticipating his pain when you break up with him, when the time is right, which it isn't yet, so you smile and take the gift, turning yourself into a big phony.

I've had so many bad Valentine's Days in my life that I'm now conditioned to hate this holiday. Like Pavlov's dog, really. When I feel it coming near, say at the beginning of February, I'm already feeling unkind. Hateful. I agree with the article—Valentine's Day is the worst, the very worst holiday. Nothing else is even a close second.

ON THE NECESSITY OF KINDNESS

Didn't feel like cooking, besides it was raining. Decided on Tony's Place—good food, quiet, cheap. Not sure why I end up eating alone so often. Working late all the time, I guess.

Sipping my chianti, I find myself drawn to a couple nearby. The man, strikingly handsome–aquiline nose, strong chin. The woman, bony shoulders, scraggly scarf like something from the sale bin at a thrift shop, mohawk on top, long wispy curls hanging down in back. Reminds me of those Make-a-Wish photos of children with cancer. She's smiling in agreement with everything he says. As they stand to go, I note her skirt, orange polka dots, hem halfway up her thigh, cute for a teenager, not a grown woman. I get a better look at his body—lithe, athletic, perfect!

I can't help thinking, why is he with this appallingly unattractive woman? Why am I alone?

The restaurant empties out, a lone waiter busses their

table, my plate of tiramisu turning gray in the darkening light. Tears inch out. Fish in my purse for a tissue, dab my face, then catch the waiter's eye. I say, my bill please.

Of course, he says. He sees my tears, he hesitates. He's an elegant young man with soft brown eyes. Do you want a box for your dessert, ma'am?

No, thank you, I say, forcing a crooked smile. Suddenly a movie, a comedy, flashes before my eyes. One character says to another, They shoot horses, don't they?

I leave a large tip. The waiter was kind. He didn't have to be, but he was.

II. LOSS

Impermanence: a reality that is hard for animal creatures such as ourselves to live with. We need, we love, we lose (and gain). But nothing, even for one moment, for one breath, remains the same.

A LETTER OF COMPLAINT

So I just learned yesterday
That my friend Jane
Is dying:
Stage IV, lung cancer.
She never smoked,
But what does that matter?

It happens all the time
Now—
They're dropping like flies—
Exactly like flies, as a matter of fact:
A short lifespan
And it's done, over, kaput.

I just want to go on record—
Not that you care—
I don't like your Plan.

Sure, it's fine for you,
Being infinite and all—
And sure, we may be

Reincarnated,
Our tiny molecules
Shifted around, atoms rearranged
Into a fish or a frog or a cat—
But to tell you the truth,
That's not much comfort,
Charlie.

Don't you understand,
Ruler of the universe,
That you plant us here,
Teach us,
After many false starts,
That love is all that matters—
And then you require that
We watch helplessly
As you thump them,
Those we love, one by one,
Like insects,
So carelessly off your plate,
Until we've nothing left.

Is that the deal, then?
To take from us
All that matters,
So that we're content to go?

Come on—
Think about it!
If in fact you think at all—
Is this a Plan
You can be proud of?
Really?

THE RED COATS ARE COMING

Attempting to stave off a growing depression, I went to the movies. It's my therapy. Big bag of popcorn, diet Pepsi, and I'm good. I hunker down, wait for images to transport me to another world. Cheaper to watch a movie at home, but not the same. I need people. In the cinema I'm aware of sounds rising all around me, people laughing, being surprised, sometimes crying softly.

I like romantic movies. Or better yet, rom-coms. Characters on the big screen get through hard times more or less in one piece—they fall in love, get betrayed, but don't die, except some of them die of cancer. Mostly people find their true love, or maybe this person was not their true love so they move on but they have grown, learned stuff. Movies are a great comfort to me.

This particular movie was one I really wasn't wild to see, about dolphins being killed for tuna fish, kind of depressing really, but I'd seen the others or didn't want to. Then I struck it lucky! I discovered a coupon for a free small popcorn in my billfold. Well, at least there's *that*, I thought. I always cough up the money for their ridiculously expensive popcorn. I am addicted, I admit. I smell the popcorn, have to have it, though I know it's stupid to spend money this way. Today, I thought, my popcorn will be free, and I will not have to eat it salted with guilt. It's popping now, oh the buttery, salty smell!

I smile as I present my coupon to the concessions girl, who has green hair and dragons running down her arms. Free popcorn! She frowns. She twists her hair. She says, I'm sorry, we can't honor this—it's expired. What? I say. I tell her what a good customer I am, how I come here all the time, why I deserve the coupon. She will not budge. I ask to see the manager.

The manager, a small man with a badge and a crisp red coat, arrives, takes the coupon, examines the expiration date. Looks at me, looks at the coupon again, looks back at me, his mouth a hard, tight line. We can't possibly honor this coupon, he says. It expired two months ago.

Why does it matter? I say.

He says, the expiration date is there so that you will keep coming.

But I do keep coming! I come here at least twice a week—in fact, I'm here right now. I just forgot that I had this coupon. My hand, clutching the coupon, begins to shake.

Sorry, I can't honor this coupon—I'll take it from you now, so you won't make this mistake again. He extends his hand to take my coupon, as if he is doing me a favor. I hand over the useless scrap of paper, like a schoolgirl caught passing notes.

He fixes his beady eyes on me. Expired means expired, he says. He wheels and is gone, red coat flashing into the dark.

HEARTSICK

This morning I was waiting for my appointment at the Medical Center, I sat next to a man of swarthy complexion. I smiled. He smiled back. We managed to chat about the weather. He had a marked accent, I couldn't place it. My eyes were drawn to a silver metal container the size of a small suitcase by his side. "What's that you got in there?" I said.

He wasn't secretive at all. "It's a tart," he said.

I laughed out loud. "Well, it's a pretty big one! What kind of tart is it? Would it be plum, or maybe peach?"

He said, "Not tart, heart. Qalb . . . qalb."

"Oh," I said, feeling silly. The silver container was the kind replacement parts are transported in—of course, a heart in the silver suitcase. . . qalb. Sits in ice, so it will live. "That's so cool!"

Amal, Amal was called on the speaker. "I must go," he said. "Doctor is waiting. I'm getting new heart."

"Hey, good luck with that!" I watched him go, the case streaming a crimson line on the shiny marble. Oh-oh, bound to be a break in his new heart. Qalb . . . qalb.

THE WOMAN WITH THIN SKIN

Came in yesterday from working in my garden, was washing off my hands and arms with good strong soap when it happened: my skin kept getting lighter in color, then thinner, then began sloughing off. The more I washed, the more skin dropped away. Tried to dry myself, but as I rubbed the towel over my body, even more skin folded and fell.

Memories came, unabated. Old hurts, in full force. A divorce a decade ago—sadness, regret for words said, words omitted. The lost child I lost, nothing to be done. An argument with my sister over inheritance. Nonsense! I should relax and read the paper. Plopped down in my lounge chair, put my feet up. Read about the war in Ukraine, soldiers freezing their sperm so that they could have babies after they were dead. Read about immigrants smothering in a truck that said MEAT on the side. Read about wildfires burning half of Canada—that's a big country to burn. Read about climate change, how time is running out. As I read, the skin on my legs began to turn loose, release the flesh, giving way to patches of nasty pink.

Must see a dermatologist! Getting an appointment would take months, though, and I was losing skin to an alarming degree. Decided to go to the emergency room, where we petitioners flopped on chairs, triaged for care. My condition was "not deemed serious," so I waited for hours.

Admitted at last to a small white room. I stripped and shivered in my flimsy flowered gown. When the young doctor saw my body, he swallowed hard, said, "I've never seen a case like this; do you have any known allergies?" He scanned his screen. It blinked, blinked at him, but couldn't help.

I said, "What if I am allergic to people? What if I'm allergic to the news?"

"Ha ha," he said, tried to smile. "You can't be allergic to everyone, everything, surely!"

"I don't know," I said. "I just know my skin is sloughing off."

"Well, there's medicine for that," he said. "I'll fix you up." I heard the hesitation in his voice, saw his eye twitch, twitch.

I held out my trembling arm, shreds of skin hanging down from it. I said, "Do you really think you can fix this?"

I caught the white in his eyes. "I don't know," he said. "I don't know."

COFFEE SHOP

Can stopping at a coffee shop change your life? Waiting in line at Starbuck's, I saw a barista so strikingly beautiful I couldn't take my eyes off her—lucent skin, dark red hair piled carelessly on top of her head, a few tendrils framing her face, lips full and sweet. And her eyes! They were a deep blue, like the ocean as night is falling. Her nametag said simply "Molly." As I stood speechless, her future unfolded before me.

Prophetic visions come to me occasionally, like they came to Grandma Rose. Grandma was known to have "the power." She could foretell the future, warn against tragic events. One evening she was resting by the fire, knitting, the needles clicking, the fire crackling in its merry way, her four children gathered round, when she suddenly dropped her knitting, leaned forward, dropped into a silence heavy as stone. She said, "James is going to call, and he's in trouble." No sooner than she spoke, the phone rang, no one moved to answer it. The children, eyes full of questions, looked at their mother. She picked up the phone only to discover that her brother James had been in a car accident. He had fallen asleep at the wheel, crossed the center line, and smashed into an oncoming car, killing the driver.

That wasn't the first time she foretold calamity, and it wasn't the last. Martha, my mother, and the other grown children have a whole raft of stories they tell. No one else from the family ever developed "the power," though, until it descended on me. I was the one gifted, condemned to carry it.

When I was about twelve, the visions started coming. Hoping they would pass, I didn't tell anyone. They did not. The first time I suspected I had the power was when I told Timmy not to ride his bike on Grangefield Road. I saw him clear as could be, lying in the mud, his bike overturned. Timmy laughed at me and rode away, but the accident happened just as I saw it: avoiding a car, he skidded out of control, was thrown off his bike. No bones broken, but a lot of bloodshed. Gravel was picked out of his flesh for days.

So I knew what was in store for Molly, this beauty serving up frappes and cappuccinos. Although I tried to push them away, the pictures came flooding in. All that she did not know, I knew.

She did not know she would reject her childhood sweetheart and marry Ellis, who saw her at the coffee shop and pursued her shamelessly until he found favor with her. She did not know she and Ellis would form an extraordinary bond of devotion, and marry. She did not know her great joy in becoming pregnant with twins, did not know she would bleed to death after she delivered them. She did not know Ellis would grieve for years and raise his daughters alone. She did not know any of this, but I knew.

Molly handed me a steaming cup of coffee, and I caught her eye. I said with all good intent and passion, "Don't marry Ellis!"

She smiled. "What did you say?"

"Please—don't marry Ellis!"

She laughed. "I don't even know anyone named Ellis."

"You will," I said.

She played along with what she thought was my little joke, a harmless way of flirting.

"Then I won't—I won't marry Ellis." She smiled and cocked her head, shaking her curls. "Who is this Ellis, anyway?"

For a moment I couldn't speak.

"Well?" she said.

I hesitated. "That's me," I said. "I'm Ellis."

I turned on my heel, walked out of the coffee shop. I never saw Molly again.

THE APOSTATE

Muffy is a special cat. I know everybody thinks their cat is special, but Muffy really is. She is part Siamese and fluffy, gray with white markings, a true beauty. I got her from the Humane Society before I met my husband Greg. She used to cuddle with me on the sofa as I graded papers, she slept close to my side at night, my arm around her soft, warm body.

Now Muffy likes Greg better than she likes me.

When Greg moved in, she started defecating on my oriental rugs. But Greg won her love by feeding her special salmon treats, bringing her cat toys. After a few months she began sidling up to him as soon as he came home. Now she prefers to cuddle on the sofa with Greg instead of me. When he is away on business, she walks the house, whining mournfully. She cries out in her sleep. Why is Greg now her one and only?

I told my best friend, Maureen, about my turncoat cat, she said, "What does it matter, who the cat likes best. It's only a damn cat." But to me, it matters. The thing is,

I'm the one who feeds her, I'm the one who cleans her litter box, I'm the one who takes her to the vet for her check-up, I'm the one who flosses her teeth, and I'm the one who bought her the fancy water dish and the scratching post. Why doesn't she love me best?

I've tried to talk with Greg about all this, he just laughs and says of course Muffy loves you best, but he's just saying that to save my feelings, I know what is true. I have bad thoughts about Muffy now, *what if I accidentally ran over her*, I would never hurt her, of course, but I can't help it, it's the way I feel. I guess it's the same with Muffy—she can't help the way she feels. She has heart trouble, just like me.

LOST AND FOUND

I'm at the Community for Earth meeting—it's my birthday. Great. Jake, my long-time boyfriend, told me last night that the relationship is over, really over—guess he didn't want to spring for a birthday gift. I feel like crawling in bed, covering up my head, not getting up, maybe ever.

The leader starts the meeting by asking everyone to tell the group something interesting about themselves. I hate this. If you say something really interesting, like I rescue abused rabbits, which I do, then people think you're bragging, so everyone says boring stuff like, I went to school with a cousin of Elvis Presley or I have a cat with six toes.

When my turn comes, I say the first thing that pops into my mind, Today is my birthday. Not a good idea, because then everyone feels obliged to sing Happy Birthday, which these not-so-good singers do. Actually, I like them singing, especially since I have no plans for my birthday. I smile and blush.

No sooner than the song is over, though, a man—

this guy has an unquenchable need for attention—says, Hey, *my* birthday is next week! As if this were a great coincidence. People say things like, Oh, really? and How about that.

Then someone else says, My birthday is next week, too! The leader says, Wow, we have a lot of April birthdays, don't we? Another member of the group says that his sister has the same birthday as his. And we're not twins! he adds. People say stuff like, Really, no kidding! Another person chimes in—If you think that's something, listen to this, I have the same birthday as my father, and my half-brother was born in Thailand exactly six years after I was born, to the day! The meeting turns into a birthday free-for-all, with everyone telling about birthdays that miraculously overlap.

That's okay, I guess. We're there mostly for social reasons, anyway. But somehow my birthday got lost. Lost and found, and lost again.

SEATTLE, IN SHADES OF GREY

based on an actual experience, names changed

Rummaging through a tiny used bookstore in an Oregon beach town, I came upon a copy of *The Collected Stories of Lydia Davis*. Opening it, I found a postcard. One side portrays the urban landscape of Seattle at night, with silver glitter on the Space Needle and on the moon. Hearts appear randomly in the sky, and twinkling stars. It reads: "Seattle, in shades of grey (sic)." On the back I found the following message:

> Dear David,
> This morning we are
> taking Ben to Fisherman's
> Terminal to look at "big
> boats" and let him run
> around a bit. Jennifer is
> on the road to Seattle.
> We all love you—commit
> to the work and come back
> to us! Love Mom

The card was addressed to David at the Lakeside-Milam Recovery Centers, in Kirkland, WA.

I am left with many questions: (1) Will David recover? (2) Who is Jennifer? (3) Will Ben be OK? (4) How broken is the heart of the mother who sent this postcard?

MY RIGHT ARM

A month ago, my right arm, the bicep, started hurting. I am healthy, a vegetarian, most vegan now. I cycle to work—6 miles there, 6 miles back, 5 days a week. I lift weights 3 days a week, have done so for 12 years. Yes, 12 years. I am very, very fit for a 59-year-old man (actually 60 next week). I thought the arm would heal quickly. Why would it not?

I woke up this morning, found my right arm still hurting. I became very angry. I thought, what is *wrong* with you, right arm? Haven't I done right by you? You ungrateful wretch! I struck it a sharp blow, said, No! Whether my arm heard or not, I don't know.

A PROPER GRASP

Maddox Derkosh, two years of age, died after falling over a wooden railing into a pit of wild African dogs at the Pittsburgh Zoo. The dogs fell upon him and he bled to death from massive wounds before his mother's eyes.

"Maddox had poor vision," his mother said. "That's why I lifted him up. He was so excited—he lunged out of my arms to see, and in a moment was gone."

"The injuries and damages sustained by Maddox," said the zoo's attorney, "were caused solely by the carelessness, negligence, and/or recklessness of Elizabeth Derkosh, who failed to maintain a proper grasp of her son."

The County DA investigated the boy's death. "The zoo is not at fault," the judge said, "nor was it the mother's fault." He said it was a "tragic accident."

Glance away, make a wrong turn, step off the edge, notice too late, turn to help, and everything is lost. We fail to maintain a proper grasp.

HOLDING ON

My cat Maggie is getting old, for a cat, she's lived almost the allotted time. That is a reality, I tell myself. A reality I don't like. You can always get another cat, people say. But I cannot get another Maggie. I cannot get a cat that was a kitten when I was with Connor. She came as we were about to end our relationship. Connor was coldhearted, but I had such passion for him. When we made love, I disappeared. No ego at all.

The day after I brought Maggie home from the Humane Society in her cardboard box—a little white ball of fuzz with blue eyes—Connor brought over a toy he had made for her, just a piece of string tied into a bow at the end. A kind gesture. He tied it to the top of a chair, we watched Maggie bat the bow around. Connor grinned. I smiled at him. Weeks after he left, his wool sports coat hung in my hall closet. I would go into the closet, bury my face in the coat, remember. It had to end, but I wanted it never to end.

THE MOST DIFFICULT SEARCH

On March 8, 2014, Malaysia Airlines Flight 370, flying from Kuala Lumpur, Malaysia, to Beijing, disappeared with 239 people aboard. At 1:19 AM, air traffic controllers lost contact with the plane. It veered suddenly from its intended path and vanished. After a long silence, the Malaysian government stated that the plane went down somewhere in the South Indian Ocean. An exhaustive international search—including 10 planes and 11 ships from more than two dozen countries—turned up nothing, not even a scrap of clothing or a fragment.

What happened? Theories abound, facts sketchy. The Boeing 777 is a big plane. It requires at least a mile to land—someone could hardly have put the big bird down on some little-known island somewhere. Australia's Prime Minister, Tony Abbott, pledged to continue the search, saying: "We owe it to the families, we owe it to everyone that travels by air."

Why this desperate searching? We want to know what happened, *we want to make sure it won't ever happen again.* On April 28, the search for debris from the missing airliner was called off, Abbott calling the 50-day effort "probably the most difficult search in human history."

Flight 370 is not the first airplane to disappear

without a trace. As a matter of fact, since 1948 more than 80 planes (capable of carrying at least 14 passengers) have been declared "missing," according to the Aviation Safety Network.

We all know the story of Amelia Earhart, the first female to fly across the Atlantic Ocean. She and her navigator, Fred Noonan, went down somewhere in the Pacific during an attempt to fly around the world. Did she run out of fuel? Land in the Philippines, as some think? *What happened?*

Then there is the dreaded Bermuda Triangle, where several ships and planes have been lost, including a squadron of five torpedo bombers in 1945. An Argentine military plane with 69 young air force cadets on board sent out an SOS at 6:00 AM on Nov. 3, 1965. It was never found. On January 30, 1979, a cargo plane bound for Rio disappeared just 30 minutes after take-off from the Tokyo International Airport. Six people were on board and 153 paintings, worth $1.2 million. It disappeared without a trace.

A photo appears in the *Wall Street Journal*, March 9, 2015. A woman whose son was on board Flight 370 is shown standing near the Malaysian Embassy in Beijing on March 8, with a handmade sign: "Mother's heart is broken, where are you my son."

III. DEATH

The flesh will not hold. But in its very failing, it teaches us to look beyond itself for meaning.

ELEGY FOR THOSE WHO CANNOT STAY

I've noticed that sometimes people decide to die,
and bless their hearts,
they find a quiet way to go,
avoiding for those left behind
the despair of suicide
with its message "you didn't love me enough"
or "now you'll be sorry."
No, those who cannot stay
generally escape with subtlety and tact,
and that's all to their credit.

I remember Bob—
Balding very early,
he slicked his hair back,
giving him an unfortunate sleazy look.
Bob always managed
to somehow miss the point—
he laughed a little too loud

when something wasn't all that funny
and then jerked his head to one side and blinked,
as if to apologize.
He seemed alone,
even in his circle of friends,
like an awkward puzzle piece
that won't quite fit,
no matter how you turn and twist it.
Bob stepped in front of a truck one day—
They said it was an accident,
tragic of course,
but after all,
so in keeping with his character.
We'll miss his funny ways, they said.

And then there was Eleanor,
in her 80s, in remarkably good health—
and she had money, lots of it,
having married wealthy men twice,
though never for love,
and had become a grateful widow.
Then her daughter Julie died,
six months after diagnosis,
and couldn't bear to see her mother at the end.
Eleanor's heart split open—
she started a torrid affair,

her first,
with a married man,
a Catholic who loved her, he said,
but could find no way to leave his wife—
I mean, my darling, when you're 85,
it's a bit too late for that, he said.
So when Eleanor started passing blood,
she didn't tell her son, or anyone,
certainly not her doctor.
She let her condition run its course,
and left strict instructions:
"Do not resuscitate!"
scotch-taped to her refrigerator door.
As she lay dying on the kitchen floor,
a friend happened by and found her there—
the last thing Eleanor said was
"Don't call 911."
She was done with joints that ached,
with fingers bent from arthritis,
done with men, I guess,
and done with loneliness.
It was sad to lose Eleanor,
people said,
but she had led a favored life,
had given lavishly to charity and church,
had dressed in unassuming elegance,

stayed thin, stood upright and proud.
A lady to the end, they said.

Another was John, a pharmacist by trade,
a quiet and sincere man,
who never got over his wife,
who left him for a series of bad boys,
which she much preferred.
John got his own place,
a modest apartment, nothing special,
not too far from her, or from his work,
and walked to and fro from the pharmacy
in good weather and in bad,
for years on end,
sometimes on Friday night
stopping for a beer at the bar.
He went out with a lady
now and then,
but no one very special.
One day chest pain arrived,
and stayed for weeks —
his grown sons said, "Daddy,
you need to do something about that—"
But John wouldn't seek a doctor's help.
He drove 200 miles to his mother's house
for a visit, nothing more,

just wanting home, I guess.
He woke in the night
in terrible pain,
slipped outside,
so as not to wake the others,
walked round and round
his childhood home,
as if the turning
would make him whole again.
Finally he stumbled in,
gasping for air, too late—
dead on arrival, they said,
and way too young.
His former wife came,
saw him still and cold—
she touched his face,
remembered his kindness,
and wept for what never was
and never could have been.

You have to hand it to them,
these ones who take their quiet leave,
so as not to inconvenience us,
making sure we're not left
with blood and guilt,
allowing us to explain their deaths,

in logical and practical terms—
inevitable, we say,
and no fault of our own.
So unassuming, so unobtrusive,
they side-step our despair,
and leave us a little innocence
to wake another day.

PLAN AHEAD

I hate it when I get postcard ads from the local crematorium. No, I don't want to "plan early" or choose a grave site—that's like inviting death, isn't it? Why focus on the negative? Whistle a happy tune, that's what I say. We know that 30% of people who receive bad test results from the doctor are reluctant to return for a conversation. Maybe if they ignore that lump in the breast or that persistent cough, it will go away. I get it, I really do.

Just doing the estate planning with my lawyer was traumatic enough, with the living will, and all that. It's easy to check off the boxes and say, *Yes, when the time comes, let me go*—because now in the healthy present, my imagination for death fails me. This is now, and that is then.

If I am lying there, totally incapacitated, somebody has to make the decision about treatment or no treatment. *Do we let her die now, or what?* my children will be asked, so to ease their decision-making, they should be informed of my wishes, the lawyer said. Yet I'm wondering who I can trust. The fact is, my children have not always appreciated my choices, like my choice to leave their father. I know they have residual anger. I have residual anger, too, but that doesn't seem to concern anyone.

I know how it goes. People become impatient with the one passing, want them to get on with it. *You can let go,* they whisper to the one who is in the last stages. *Don't worry about us, you can let go.* What they really mean is, *Will you please go ahead and die, for god's sake, I have to take the kids to soccer practice all next week, there's a tournament coming up.* I don't mean to be cynical, but I've seen it happen.

I am in my condo overlooking the river. Usually it's quiet, peaceful. But today a maintenance man with an electric scythe, a not-so-grim reaper, is beginning work just outside my window, three stories down. Rrrrr, RRRR, Rrrrr. He is a young man, brown and muscular, with a funny orange hat. Absolutely focused. The scream is relentless. The trend is clear. For him, I do not exist. Not for him, not for others. One day. Not.

THE QUEST(S)

based on facts from
"Deliverance From 27,000 Feet,"
by John Branch
(*NYTimes*, Dec. 19, 2017)

—A poster of Mt. Everest has been on the bedroom wall of the modest home of Gontam Ghosh, a Bengali policeman, for twenty years. Conquering Everest has been the lifelong dream of Ghosh and three other Bengalis—Nath, Paul, and Hazra. The four scrimp and save for over ten years to make the climb. They finally have enough to go on a "low budget" expedition, much cheaper than those contracted by wealthier Americans and Europeans. They have four Nepalese sherpas.

—On May 20, 2016, Ghosh, Paul, Nath, and Hazra are relaxing in a tent at Camp 4. After so much time at Base Camp, on the lower parts of Everest, they are close to their goal. They drink cups of tea, eat crackers, hardly speak at all. Hopefully, everything will go as planned—in 24 hours they will have returned to Camp 4, heading home. Back in India, they will be heroes, "Everesters," as the locals called them.

—The four climbers and their guides, for some inexplicable reason, start their climb after dark. Climbers rarely start later than noon.

—Bishnu Gurung, the only one of their guides to have ever reached the summit, gets a radio message from the Base Camp manager, recommending that the four Bengali climbers turn back.

—Ghosh weeps when he considers returning. He, Paul, and Hazra persist, in spite of the warning. Their supply of oxygen is growing dangerously low. Only Nath chooses to return to Camp 4.

—Paul Pottinger, a doctor from Seattle, reaches the summit at 7:48 that morning. As he is climbing down, he passes Paul and his guide still ascending. Concerned, he repeatedly warns the guide of the time.

—Gurung, Ghosh's guide, leaves him at the South Summit and continues to climb. He takes pictures of himself 21 times at what seems to be the summit.

—An American climber, Thom Pollard, along with his Nepali guide leave for a summit attempt. They pass two cold and frightened sherpas who have no more oxygen. They see two climbers, Hazra and Ghosh. Ghosh's gloves are off, he is lying on his side, he appears near death. Pollard and his guide decide to continue up the mountain.

—On his way down, Pollard sees Ghosh again. He is alone. He is dead. Pollard steps over Ghosh, continues down. Later Pollard says he continues to be haunted by his decision.

—Leslie Binns, a British climber, ascending above Camp 4, finds Hazra, her mittens off, her jacket open. He gives her a shot of oxygen, aborts his summit climb, saves her life. Another expedition sees Paul, takes him to Camp 4. He dies there in a tent.

—News reports erroneously claim that the four climbers have reached the summit of Everest. Families and friends rejoice, share Bengali sweets.

—Two other Sherpas search, find Nath's body. They know it's Nath because he is the climber with only one hand. Weather conditions keep the sherpas from going higher to look for Ghosh. The climbing season is over. The bodies of Ghosh and Nath are left on the mountain.

—Ghosh's wife, Chandana, keeps wearing red and white bracelets on her right wrist, a sign that she is married. She believes Ghosh is still alive. Without a death certificate, Chandana has no access to Ghosh's pension from his job as a police officer.

—Ghosh's family are devout Hindus. They believe that without cremation, the soul cannot be reincarnated. They desperately want his body returned.

—Ghosh's brother Debasish raises money to pay experienced climbers to recover the body. The family sells a small lot, jewelry, including some Chandana wore on her wedding day. Debasish collects savings from the extended family and members of the local mountaineering club.

—Five sherpas chip out Gontam Ghosh's body from ice near the summit of Mt. Everest, where it has lain for over a year. The body is contorted, the face black. Ghosh was 50 years old when he died. His body is returned home.

—Nepal officials say around two hundred bodies remain at various points on Everest. Some become gruesome markers for other climbers. Most can't be seen, having been thrown off cliffs or into crevasses. Dead bodies are not good for the tourist trade.

THE DEER

Walking the dusty road at dusk
I came upon the carcass
of a young deer.
I stooped to look.

It was a fresh kill,
red flesh still clinging
to a cage of bones.
The head was intact,
the white-tipped tail as well,
but little else remained.
Just bones and scattered tufts of hair.

I imagine my end so different:
a comfortable bed,
surrounded by grieving family and friends,
a quiet, pain-free trip to light.
Not like the deer,
Eyes frozen open in wonder,
as if to say, oh really, my time is here?

LOADED

"Big Game Hunter Killed
by Elephant in Zimbabwe"
(*NYTimes*, May 22, 2017)

According to the Afrikaans media outlet Netwerk 24, a professional big game hunter, Theunis Botha, 51, was killed by an elephant. Apparently, a group of hunters suddenly came across a breeding herd of elephants. Three cows stormed the hunters, Botha shot at them. A fourth cow then stormed them from the side, lifting Botha with her trunk. A member of the hunting party shot the elephant, the fatally wounded creature falling onto Botha, crushing him to death.

Botha, who owned a company called Game Hounds Safaris, led leopard and lion hunting safaris with his large pack of dogs. The dogs drive the animals toward hunters who then open fire. Botha often travelled to the US to recruit wealthy Americans for trophy hunting. Supporters of big game hunting say that the sport boosts tourism, helps conservation efforts by raising the value of wildlife.

A spokesperson from the Elephant Listening Project said that a phenomenon known as "mating pandemonium" has been documented for at least 25 years. Female elephants mate only once every four years, he said. "When a cow goes into estrus, she makes a loud rumbling sound. She chooses a mate and as they copulate, the entire elephant family surrounds them, even the calves, trumpeting loudly and running circles around them to cheer them on. Clearly these hunters were not invited to the party."

A Zimbabwean game warden investigating the incident agreed, saying, "Anyone entering another's bedroom during mating is fair game. The elephant should be held blameless." A native bystander concurred, saying Botha was not killed by the elephant, but rather was killed by the friend who shot the elephant. "This tragic death was accidental," he said, "for Botha's friend did not know that the elephant was loaded."

A FERVENT WISH

I just want to get out of this world without doing something really stupid. We all blunder into stuff—get a little drunk, or look the wrong way, or at the wrong person, and whamo! For some, it happens young, like the five-year-old who shot his sister. "Uh-oh," he said, and put the pistol down. He could grow up to be a bank president or saint, but people will always whisper, "Did you know he shot his sister?"

Or the man who died trying to capture a grizzly on video in Glacier National Park. The signage was clear: DO NOT LEAVE YOUR VEHICLE. "This is a great shot!" he said. "The bear is there!" All the while his wife is begging him, "Herman, get back in the car!" It's all on video tape. Friends will send friends the link to the article, will tell the story for years to come: "Did you hear about the man who got eaten by a bear? I knew him—the man, I mean."

And then there was the high school teacher who fell in love with his sixteen-year-old student. It happens. He ran off with her, leaving his pregnant wife and two children behind, in Utah, which is a bad state for loving someone who is underage, especially if you have a pregnant wife. He got sent up for twelve long years. His wife forgave him, the state didn't. Does anyone remember now that he was "Teacher of the Year" for three years running, or that he went back home and raised his kids? "What was he *thinking?*" people will say, and they'll speculate about the girl, who never saw him again. They say she became a lawyer.

You try to do the right thing, to be good, like your mama said—I mean, unless you are the serial killer type. But then one summer day the sun streaks in and blinds you, and before you know it, whoosh, you've done that one unforgivable deed, taken that single misstep in the long march of days that defines you for good, the one stupid thing that people will remember, and believe that's all you are.

HALLELUJAH, REDUX

It's Easter Sunday. Three doors down from our house, Rosie, a little three-year-old and her mom are looking for Easter eggs in their back yard when Francie, the mom, notices a pair of tennis shoes sticking out from the crawl space under the deck. She calls the police. They "investigated discreetly," the paper reports, and found a body. Francie says she had noticed "a foul smell," but couldn't figure out where it was coming from—until the Easter egg hunt. Rosie never learns that a dead man was under their house.

I am twelve years old, living with my grandparents in Homer, a little town in N. Louisiana. Easter Sunday is my time to wear a new dress (pastel) to church, new shoes (patent leather), and new gloves (white). Grownup ladies are wearing hats with big brims. The church is packed; we sit there like rows of spring flowers in our new array. The choir, in maroon robes with gold satin stoles, sings *up from the grave He arose*. The minister talks about how death isn't the end for those who are saved, that there is a place of glory waiting for us. Jesus rose from the dead, and we will, too. His voice fills with emotion, catches in his throat. We sing *Hallelujah*.

FACTS ABOUT HOUSEFLIES

—Female flies are prolific. They lay 9,000 eggs in their short lifetime. The larvae, little wrigglers called maggots, hatch within a day, and begin consuming whatever is around. They prefer dead animals or feces, but any old garbage will do. Within three days or so, they become flies.

—Around 36 hours after leaving the pupa stage, the female is ready to mate. The male mounts her from behind, taking only a few seconds, or a couple of minutes for more relational partners. The female has to mate just once, for she can store the sperm for later use (handy!). Unlike geese, flies do not mate for life.

—Through the study of flies, scientists have discovered secrets of aging. They found that DNA damage (8-OHdG) makes houseflies get old. The more DNA damage, the shorter the life span, a conclusion which has the ring of truth about it.

—The reason you have great difficulty killing houseflies is that their metabolism is much faster than yours, so you seem to move in slow motion to them. Thus, the frustrated, "Gotcha! Damn."

—Dr. Erica McAlister, a research scientist, has captured her affection for flies in a book, *The Secret Lives of Flies*. McAlister reminds us of the importance of flies to humanity—they are not just something to swat. She says, "I love them. They do everything. They get everywhere. They're noisy. And they love having sex."

—Film buffs and fly aficionados love *The Fly*, a science-fiction movie by director David Cronenberg, starring Jeff Goldblum and Geena Davis. Goldblum turns into a fly (accident!) and Davis, his lover, dreams of giving birth to a giant maggot, one of the most thoroughly disgusting scenes in cinema history.

—Also, film lovers might wish to see *Eega*, a Telugu film, the story of the revenge of a housefly. Director SS. Rajamouli, of India, said, "When I say I am making a film about a housefly, there will be wonder, smile. Some will be heckling and thinking has he gone mad?" Because the film is in Telugu, a South-Central Dravidian language, primarily spoken in Andhra Pradesh, India, the film had a multilingual release. Though not widely screened, it nevertheless created a lot of buzz.

A GOOD DEATH

"What an elegant couple!" I thought
when we first met,
both erect, both with luminous white hair,
so alive in the world.
Their time began winding down, though,
as time will do—
Robert ravaged with cancer,
Alice staying close beside.
"Will you come?"
she asks of me,
and I do,
though I was dreaming of lying in the sun,
somewhere far away.

I walk into the white and metal room,
Robert greets me with his silver smile,
and for a moment
I imagine him whole,
but no,
he has his own agenda.

The nurse arrives to change his wound,
I get up to go,
because who wants to look death in the face.
"No, stay," says Alice,
"I want to share my pain."

I watch the nurse
peel back the bed clothes,
remove the gown,
I see white tape
the size of a dinner plate.
She gently tugs and tugs,
he winces with the pain,
til off the white patch comes,
revealing a rotting mass of flesh,
a cavernous hole,
yellow-white and red.
The smell of death fills the air,
gorge rises in my throat.

Two days later he dies,
Six months after, she follows.
He was her high-school sweetheart,
flesh of her flesh,
heart of her heart.

Do you find in this story
some bittersweet redemption?
Are you going to tell me
That they are better off now,
Or together, still, in death,
Or that their love inspires
Those who remain?
Do you want to make something pretty of this,
or good?
Go ahead,
then tell me how you did it.

THE REVENGE OF THE WHALE

based on a true story

A sperm whale was beached on the Oregon coast, near Seaside. The few townspeople and all the tourists went to see the whale, which was 45 feet long and weighed about eight tons. The corpse was quite an attraction for the first few days, but as it began to decay and bloat up, it became less popular, except with the most adventurous children. After 5 days, even they were turned away by the putrid smell. The carcass was filling with gas. What if it should explode?

The city called in the Oregon Department of Transportation (ODOT), and one of their engineers, a young innovator, came up with an ingenious plan: they would dynamite the whale to smithereens, and the small pieces would fall to the beach, where the fragments of flesh would be consumed by seagulls and crabs, thus completing the cycle of life. He argued that his plan was ecologically sound and consistent with Oregon values.

ODOT agreed, the dynamite obtained. However, there is very little literature on "blowing up whales," so our feckless engineer did not know how much dynamite to use. "Nothing ventured, nothing gained," he said. "We have to think out of the box." He made his best estimate, placing the charge on the beach side of the whale, hoping that most of the carcass would end up in the water.

Not much was happening in Seaside, as per usual, so by the time ODOT was ready to set off the dynamite, a sizable crowd had gathered. For safety's sake, these onlookers were cordoned off about ¼ mile away from the site. A television crew from Portland came in to record the event.

The countdown began.

The blast was mighty, sending red, orange, and yellow streams and great clouds of smoke into the sky. *Oh-h-h-h!* the crowd exclaimed. It was like the Fourth of July. But the blast was not quite mighty enough. Large chunks of whale began falling from the sky, pelting not only the ODOT workers but also the crowd of onlookers. People began scattering, throwing their arms over their heads. Frightened children ran to their mothers. One chunk of flesh was massive enough to crush the top of a brand-new Cadillac owned by one of the town fathers, which he fortunately was not in. People were covered with rotting blubber, foul-smelling grease, and yellow spinal matter oozing from the vertebrae of the whale. Screams, groans, and profanity rose from the crowd. Dogs howled, sea gulls cried, sirens sounded.

Whale parts invaded Seaside, once a pleasant respite from city life. Whale entrails were draped over a neon sign EAT HERE, at the entrance of a popular restaurant. Chunks of whale heart fell in the grass in front of the Love Nest B&B. Whale lungs, still partially inflated, blocked the entrance to the Balloon and Kite Shop. The Reader's Roost, a bookstore and coffee house, had to deal with a whale penis, an organ which is larger than one might think. The young traffic engineer was fired and moved far, far away.

That was back in 1970. Seaside has never been quite the same. If you go there to visit, you will soon hear the whispers, see the sideways glances among the townsfolk—that is, those who had the stomach to remain. Their eyes growing big, they will begin, *Have you heard about the whale?*

CHRISTMAS HARD ON DOGS

Taken from various print and online sources,
12/14/17 to 12/17

Bethany Lynn Stephens, 22, didn't arrive home when her father expected her. He went out looking for her in the woods where she generally walked her dogs. He found the dogs, two pit bulls, guarding what he initially thought was an animal carcass.

Sadly, this was not the case—the remains were that of his daughter Bethany. Sheriff James Askew, of Goochland County, Virginia, said in his first public report, "Stephens was being, for lack of a better term, *guarded* by two very large brindle-colored pit bull dogs." He added that initial findings from the medical examiner confirmed that Stephens's wounds were "consistent with being mauled by these dogs."

People in the community could not believe that Bethany's pets had killed her. Maybe she had been attacked and raped. Maybe her dogs were protecting her. Perhaps Stephens might have been mauled by a wolf or a bear, some suggested. The findings from the medical examiner claimed that "the bite wounds were inconsistent with the bite strength of a larger animal."

Finally, in order to settle the doubts floating around, Sheriff Askew made a definitive statement to the press. He paused for an inordinately long time before speaking: "I and four other deputy sheriffs observed the dogs eating the rib cage on the body." He further said that Stephens had incredibly traumatic wounds to her arms, chest, and face.

The dogs were euthanized. "I think it was in the best interest of our community and for public safety to do that," Askew said. "Once a dog tastes human flesh, it's no longer safe to have that dog around humans." He said he had "no idea" what caused the attack, but "I can tell you that since this happened, I've spent a significant amount of time researching attacks by dogs of this sort, and while it is not an everyday occurrence, it is not rare."

Studies, in fact, support Askew's contention. According to research compiled by Merritt Clifton, the editor of *Animals 24-7*, an animal news organization, pit bulls make up only 6% of the dog population, but they are responsible for 68% of dog attacks and 52% of dog-related deaths since 1982. The *Annals of Surgery* reported that one person is killed by a pit bull every fourteen days, and that there is a "higher risk of death than are attacks from other breeds."

Pamela Reid, Ph.D., vice-president of the ASPCA's animal behavior center, doesn't agree with this assessment. Reid says that pit bulls are not aggressive with people, but they have "great tenacity—they put their mind to something and they do it." She notes that "Petey" from *The Little Rascals* was a pit bull, and that Helen Keller, Theodore Roosevelt, and Fred Astaire all had pit bulls. Reid claims that some pit bulls "are absolutely lovely with other animals—cats and bunnies—but others are not." She advises, "Take introductions slowly."

Like Reid and other pit bull advocates, Jim Gorant, the author of *Lost Dogs*, places the responsibility for pit bull attacks squarely on the owners. He says, "Every dog is an individual. Pit bulls are just dogs and if they are not properly raised and socialized and treated right, they can have behavior problems." One of the deputies, Sgt. Mike Blackwood, concurred, regarding the Stephens case. The dogs "were a bit neglected," Blackwood said. "She left the dogs with her father . . . and so they became more isolated. They became a little distant from their owner towards the end."

A further consideration, and perhaps the key to this young woman's tragic death: Bethany was killed during the Christmas season. Dog behaviorist and trainer Carolyn Menteith notes that "many dog bites occur during the holiday season, with the house full of guests, children excited, walks neglected, leaving the dog bored and confused." She says that Christmas can be hard on dogs.

We all know that Christmas can be hard on people, but how many of us understand how devastating Christmas can be for dogs? We neglect our pets at our peril.

IV. TRUTH

In our postmodern world, truth has become relative. There is only your story, your truth, and my story, my truth. Where are the human values that cross philosophical and theological lines, values that give our lives integrity, meaning, and purpose? Without God or state or science or authority, we float free, with no rudder.

NOT A PROBLEM

Marion is a worrier, always has been. Her mother, constitutionally happy, told her at age 3, "Don't be a worrywart, little daughter." But worry was part of Marion's destiny. She is now 73 years old. She worries about the unattractive spots which are appearing on her skin, she worries about the loud music coming from the house next door, she worries about the rattle in her car, she worries about the ulcer on her cat's neck, she worries because the weather is cold and rainy, she worries that because of her bunions she will never find shoes she likes, she worries that the grocery will have no more radicchio, she worries that her cleaning lady is stealing restricted drugs from her bathroom, she worries because she is constipated, she worries because her good friend got married and never calls her anymore.

One evening as Marion was sautéing some onions, her heart stopped. As she fell to the floor, clutching a wooden spoon, she understood that she would never have to worry again.

JUST PASSING BY

A scruffy looking man is sitting on a park bench. A puppy is swimming frantically toward him, in a shallow pool of water left by a recent rain. The puppy is whimpering and has floppy ears. When the puppy reaches the man, he throws the puppy back into the water. He does so again and again, and each time the puppy swims back to him. Finally the puppy can swim no more, and drowns.

There is photographer on the scene, capturing the story. He is a professional and snaps many pictures from various points of view: bending, kneeling, standing. The one he judges best will be in the newspaper the next day. Many people will be moved by the image of the puppy struggling to live. They will wonder how the man on the bench could be so cruel. They will not want to believe, as a reporter states in the caption to this picture, that the puppy drowns. They will think that perhaps someone, some stranger, will rescue the puppy, somehow. That will not be so.

The photographer does not try to save the puppy. That is not his role. He is an observer. He was just noticing, just passing by.

NEW GLASSES

I got my new glasses today, but I realized when I started wearing them, that I do not want to see this clearly. So I'm not going to.

POLECAT

People are crazy about their dogs. So I am talking with my best friend last week—she has this dog named Polecat who got its name when it was a pup and faced down a skunk in the back yard, barking and barking. The dog is . . . I wouldn't say ugly, but I wouldn't say attractive, either. I mean if I was gonna get a dog—which I'm not, because they're too much trouble—I would get a pretty one, like an Afghan. I saw one in the city once, it was silver all over, and walked like a prince. Its face was kindly, with dark eyes and curly hair parted in the middle and hanging down like rivulets, reminding me for the world, of my grandmother. If I was gonna get a dog, I would like one that is so beautiful it makes me happy whenever I look at it. Esthetics is important.

Anyway, my friend's dog is about as ordinary as they come—short hair, tan with a long stringy tail, and a white spot on his chest. Ordinary as sin. But of course Polecat is absolutely devoted to her. She's single—I think that's why she's so attached to this dog. She had a boyfriend, actually a whole series of them, but none of them stuck. Polecat sticks, you have to say that for him.

So she's talking about Polecat, scratching his ears, and ruffling his fur, and saying, "Good dog, good dog," and things like that, and then she says, "Polecat is my child." Well, that was too much for me. I have a child, and a dog is not a child.

So I say to her, "Your dog is not your child. Your dog is a dog." She's offended of course and says her dog means everything to her and who was I to say. I just wanted to make my case plain enough for anyone to see, so I say, "Well, who would you like to get run over by a car—your dog, or your sister?" She hesitates, so I say, "OK, I know you never liked your sister. What about me? Would you like me to get run over, or your dog?" I thought I had her there. But she hesitated again. I couldn't believe it. She said, "Either one would be a tragedy."

So putting two and two together, I can see I don't have any more worth than a dog to her. Or maybe I have as much worth to her as her dog. That's a better way to look at it, I guess. She sure loves that dog.

ADDICTED TO TRUTH

When I was four years old, Mother found my tiny fingerprints in her freshly baked lemon meringue. I said, Daddy did it! I got quite a spanking for that. This is my earliest memory.

I've always been addicted to truth. People ask, How are you? It is a polite inquiry, that's all, yet I find I'm compelling to say how I really am, which sometimes isn't so good.

Grocery clerks ask these days, How's your day going? Puts me in a tight spot. I say, Great, then feel guilty because I have evaded the truth.

The Friday after a particularly trying Thanksgiving. I went to a favorite restaurant, alone, the way I wanted it. Right off, the hostess says, How did your holiday go? I said, Not very well. Clearly thrown off her game, she said, Oh, and showed me to a table in the corner by the kitchen.

People in my condo try to be pleasant, greet others in the elevator. Recently a man with, I have to say, an adorable dog made eye contact and said, How are you? I said, I am sad, I just left the bedside of a dying friend.

Maybe I should not have said what I said but I could not say, Just fine, because I was not even remotely fine. He looked away, mumbled I'm sorry as he and his dog left. Even the dog looked downcast.

A dear friend invited me to a new Thai restaurant to celebrate my birthday, she said it was fabulous. It was not fabulous, not even good. How do you like the food, she asked, expectantly. What could I do—lie to my friend? I hesitated, finally said, It's . . . *different*. Her face fell. I didn't want to hurt my friend, but I did.

Maybe I should go into recovery, give up my addiction. Maybe there's a choice between truth and love. Maybe loving has lying built in.

THE REVOLT
OF THE STOMACHS

My husband and I wanted to welcome the new restaurant into our neighborhood. It's hard to start a restaurant, especially one with a name like Noraneko. I guess it's Japanese; the review said it means "alley cat."

We showed up a week or two after the opening. The interior was dark, with shiny black tables. When our eyes adjusted, we saw abstract pictures of orange and blue fish covering the walls. The menu featured things like fifteen versions of ramen and something they called "sushi cheese"—just like sushi, except it's cheese not fish, the waiter said—we stock the cheese bar with thirty different kinds of "sushi quality" cheeses. The special was steak tartare topped with a partially cooked egg, sprinkled with sushi cheese.

We wanted to support the new owner, but our stomachs did not want to. They hesitated, then they insisted. So we left.

ORDERING, MY LIFE

I hear people in the condo mailroom complain, Oh, just a bunch of catalogs. But I like catalogs, I like ordering. I don't go much of anywhere, except to the grocery and now and then, a movie.

I have a method. I make myself a cup of tea, sit down in my easy chair, look through my new catalogs. My favorites are Poetry, Wrap, Garnet Hill, Eileen Fischer, Neiman Marcus, and of course Nordstrom's. When I see an item I like, I turn under that page. I rarely buy anything on first look, later I might have another look, say to myself, Whoa, what was I thinking! Or I might realize I have something just like it, or similar.

I like ordering because when I get a package notice, I feel excited. I wonder, *what is it?* It is an actual surprise, because usually I have forgotten what I ordered. It's like getting a gift when you didn't expect it from somebody who knows what you like. I go pick up my package, take it to my unit, and tear into it like a kid.

I read an article on hoarding recently. I am not a hoarder at all, but I do have a lot of clothes that I don't wear. The article advised, give away any article of clothing you haven't worn for two years. Makes sense, make room for the new. So I did. I filled three large boxes, then started thinking about the clothes again, you never know when you might need that black Vera Wang jacket. Or those NYDJ jeans that have always been too tight. What if I got sick and lost weight? I would want those very jeans. Besides, they were expensive.

I didn't take my clothes to Goodwill. I couldn't. Two months later, they're still in the trunk of my car, kind of a halfway house for clothing in transition. Like me. Unclear as to when they will be released.

DO NOT DISTURB

Ben wanted to marry Liz, he couldn't his parents said because she came from bad blood, he wanted to study history, he couldn't because there's no money in history, he married quite the right girl from a good family, became a banker, produced a boy and a girl, did very well indeed, one evening in the garage attached to his well-appointed home he gassed himself quietly to death so as not to disturb anyone, he didn't leave a note, there was nothing left to say.

READING LYDIA DAVIS

I got a copy of *The Complete Works of Lydia Davis*, as I am intrigued by her writing. It is a very fat book, over 2 inches thick and 731 pages long. Part of the length is excusable, for the book is only 7 inches tall and 4 1/2 inches wide, making it a short, fat book, not a tall, wide fat book.

Still I wonder at Lydia Davis's choice to include her *complete* works. As every writer knows, some pieces we publish are better than others, the others being inferior to the better ones. Davis would have been better served to choose the better pieces, maybe half as many, which would have made the very orange and fat book more aesthetically pleasing and easier to read while eating a grilled cheese sandwich and/or a bowl of tomato soup. She could have named this reduced volume *Many of the Works of Lydia Davis* or *The Works of Lydia Davis That She Likes Best*—or, in a more humble vein, *Some of the Works of Lydia Davis*, or even *A Few of the Better Works of Lydia Davis*.

As for where to cut, I would suggest omitting at least half of her longer stories, e.g., "Mrs. D and Her Maids," which is clever but excessive at 28 pages, or "We Miss

You: A Study of Get-Well Letters from a Class of Fourth-Graders," which I find both charming and poignant, but I think most readers will agree becomes tedious long before reaching the end of the 27 pages of letters. Even the title is too long.

Of course, I could stop reading the longer pieces before I finish, but then because I did not finish, I would not know the end, and ends are often the most significant parts of her stories, or anyone's, so I trudge on to the end, then often find that the end just keeps on going and doesn't end at all, thus frustrating my need for resolution.

I quite like Davis's very short pieces—I can read them quickly, since they are not nearly as long as her long pieces. Some are only one sentence long and therefore extremely short. I need not drop my spoon or my sandwich for these. I can just say, "Ah!" or "Well done!" and feel satisfied. The advantage of the short pieces is that I can read more stories at one sitting, and reading more stories that I like instead of fewer that I don't like as much makes me feel that I have accomplished more, which I like very much.

DEATH RISES LIKE
A DINOSAUR OUT
OF THE DUCK POND

title from "Extended Care,"
by Michael Ryan

The doctor said in answer to my hapless question, *no one knows how long everyone is different, I've known those who've gone as long as six months or more, but the more is not years, it's months.* I don't believe it, not possible to be me then not me, my Buddhist friends say there is no me anyway, they believe in reincarnation, not all that logical when you consider how many of us there are to reincarnate, I wish I could buy it, but *my* breath is the one to become ragged, *my* heart to stop, *my* body to dress and take to the boneyard or to be eaten by fire. When the talk about the weather stops, when the talk about the President stops, when the talk about the big pigskin game stops, when the talk turns to those dying or dead, as it eventually does, someone will smile, will say, *I'm not afraid of death*—used to be me, ha, turns out that's a crock.

MY FEARLESS MORAL INVENTORY

The Adult Child meeting has a theme, and the theme this week was #4 on their 12-step program: "Make a searching and fearless moral inventory." I try very hard to be a good person—so I didn't see why I should do any kind of "moral inventory." Still, I feel guilty about not being good enough—anyway, that's another problem I have, guilt. But then Joanie, she's been in the program for a while, explained that I am unhappy for a reason, and I need to consider what I'm doing to make myself unhappy, as she put it. She said, "Just try the inventory and see what happens." Call me if you get stuck. OK, so this is what I came up with:

My Fearless Moral Inventory

1. I don't send birthday cards to people I should remember on their birthday.

2. I tell people they really look good when they don't, so they will feel better.

3. I have a really messy desk, which results in losses of bills occasionally.

4. I tear out pages of recipes from magazines in the waiting room of my doctor and dentist.

5. I have violent thoughts about people I don't like.

6. I am judgmental, especially about fat people.

7. I am almost always late for appointments, but I hate it if others are.

8. I have been known to write (in pencil) in library books.

9. I yell at bad drivers—not all the time, but sometimes, usually when I'm running late.

10. I wear my underwear 2 days in a row, occasionally more.

11. I pick wildflowers in designated wilderness preserves, but not many.

12. I pass trash on the sidewalk in my neighborhood and don't pick it up.

13. I feel jealous if another woman looks really pretty and I don't that day.

14. I am not a racist, but sometimes I have racist thoughts, especially about Black people.

15. I am greedy at buffet tables and take more shrimp than my share.

16. My sister drives me crazy at times, and I tell her, which is unkind.

17. When I'm supposed to read everything on a legal agreement and sign when I have, I sign without reading it.

18. I notice men's penis sizes, which is disrespectful.

19. I sometimes feel like hurting small and helpless animals, like little barking dogs.

20. I talk about myself too much, and on the other hand, don't want to listen to other people, especially when they talk about their grandchildren or their vacations.

I think I will stop here, as this list could be endless, but you get the idea. I have a ways to go. I'm not sure these meetings will make me make better choices. You'll see, Joanie says. So OK, I'm going to try it.

HOPE SPRINGS ETERNAL

God woke up, stretched, and yawned, and decided to start on His next project, a new being. He wanted to create something really special this time. God's assistant, Murray, said, "Been there, done that. Remember how homo sapiens turned out?"

God remembered, and God became dejected. "OK, I know, I know," He said. We'll have to build in more controls this time. The earth project turned out to be a colossal mess—embarrassing!"

"I'll say," said Murray. "The explosion will be reverberating through time forever."

"Yeah," said God. "I think the free will thing was a big mistake."

"So you're going for AI, programming them all?"

"No," mused God. "No, that would be no fun." God paused thoughtfully, then continued, "I think . . . I think I'll have them evolve into beings who love everyone—you know, everyone the same. That way there'll be no wars, no starvation, no racism, sexism, ageism, etc."

And so God began. He created what He called the Beloved Community. There was no greed, no envy, no competition, no conquering—and best of all, no fear.

One day some eons later Murray said, "Have you checked out the pure love group lately?"

"No, as a matter of fact. Thanks for the reminder. Next Thursday, it's on my schedule."

But when God visited, he was chagrined. He saw in his new creation no yearning, no curiosity. And of course, no devotion. They were a complacent herd of sheep, with no need for God. "Damn," said God. "I forgot to include desire."

"Yeah, you really screwed up," said Murray.

"I have to agree—what an oversight! Nothing to do but let go."

"And this time, don't send an ark."

And so God made rain to fall 40 days and 40 nights, and a great water covered the planet. God was tempted to send an ark, because He loved all his creations, even this one. But He thought better of it: "No, with this kind of design flaw, there's no way to correct." God sighed. "I'll just have to start over."

Murray said, "I know you meant well, God. But hey—think it through next time."

ACKNOWLEDGEMENTS

"A Letter of Complaint," *Oregon Literary Review*

"Not a Problem," *Spank the Carp, 2020 Anthology*

"Tree of Life" and "The Dancer," *Dash*, Literary Review, Spring 2021

"A Fervent Wish," "A Proper Grasp," and "Hope Springs Eternal," in *Elderberries*, newsletter of the Unitarian Universalist Retired Members and Partners Association, Fall 2023.

9 780099 610408 1